The Salmon Who Dared

Ahn Do-hyun is a multi-million bestselling, award-winning Korean poet. He was born in 1961 in Yeocheon, Korea, and graduated from Wonkwang University where he studied Korean literature. His writing career took off when he won the Daegu Maeil Shinmun Annual Literary Contest with his poem 'Nakdong River' in 1981 and the Dong-A Ilbo Annual Literary Contest with his poem 'Jeon Bong-jun Goes to Seoul' in 1984. Ahn also received the 1996 Young Poet's Award and the 1998 Kim So-wol Literature Prize. This is his first work to be translated into English.

AHN DO-HYUN

The Salmon Who Dared
to Leap Higher

PAN BOOKS

First published in 1996 by Munhakdongne Publishing Corp., Korea, under the title *Yeon eo*

This edition first published 2015 by Pan Books
an imprint of Pan Macmillan, a division of Macmillan Publishers Limited
Pan Macmillan, 20 New Wharf Road, London N1 9RR
Basingstoke and Oxford
Associated companies throughout the world
www.panmacmillan.com

ISBN 978-1-4472-6999-1

1 3 5 7 9 8 6 4 2

A CIP catalogue record for this book is available from the British Library.

Printed and bound by CPI Group (UK) Ltd, Croydon, CR0 4YY

Visit **www.panmacmillan.com** to read more about all our books
and to buy them. You will also find features, author interviews and
news of any author events, and you can sign up for e-newsletters
so that you're always first to hear about our new releases.

I dedicate this book
To those who believe
Hope and love
Still exist in this world –
A love that is used like a rag
Only good for discarding
But which nobody can give up,
On the contrary, this love we want
To experience it even if only that once again –
Those who see within it their reason for living

'Salmon: the very word is heady with the scent of the rushing river.'

The short piece I wrote, which begins with that line, became entangled in a mesh of difficulties, every bit as tricky to escape as a fisherman's net. It tells the story of the salmon conservation movement in Korea, set up by fishermen in response to the dangerously low number of salmon which successfully return to the rivers of their birth, such as the Great Southern Stream. Once the magazine featuring the story started to appear in bookshops, I began to receive a number of unexpected phone calls from readers calling to complain.

The first caller announced straight off that he was an environmentalist, then launched into a diatribe against the selfishness of human beings:

destroyers of the ecosystem. On the other end of the line, I found myself nodding in agreement. He was working himself up into a fierce passion, but he was clearly sincere – a rare quality – and so I chose not to interrupt. Instead, I stood there in silence and gave him my humble attention. All of a sudden, though, he began to pick fault with the title of my piece, which was 'How to Enjoy Salmon Fishing'. Before I had the chance to say anything in my defence, the caller abruptly concluded that I was nothing more than a piece of human trash, and unceremoniously hung up. The whole episode left me somewhat at a loss. More than likely he'd only picked up the magazine so as to have some reading material for the bathroom; rather than giving my piece a thorough read, he'd probably done nothing more than flick through the table of contents. I really couldn't understand how anyone could make up their mind about me on the basis of the title alone. I guess nothing beats humans when it comes to impatience.

Another caller took issue with the very first line, which I'd inserted as a kind of epigraph. According to him, to say that salmon give off the scent of the river was taking artistic licence too far, the kind of idiocy only a writer would dream up. Salmon spend ten times as much of their lives in the sea as they do in rivers, he explained, and so the expression I'd used was contradicted by biological fact. A more accurate expression, he suggested, would be something like 'Salmon – the very word is redolent of the teeming sea'. This was all fair enough, but the caller seemed to be somewhat lacking in imagination. Such people don't tend to realize the importance of the bigger picture.

All this made me decide to rewrite my article. In order to avoid any more misunderstandings on the part of the reader, I gave it a simpler title.

I wanted to find out all there was to know about salmon, and my first ports of call were an encyclo-paedia and an illustrated guide to fish. From these, I gleaned the following information: the pull of the stream of their birth draws salmon upriver every year from September to November, the months when the turning leaves dye the mountainsides a riotous palette of crimson and gold; in the shallows, where the current is sluggish, female salmon use their tails to dig holes in the gravelly riverbed; these holes are approximately 1m across and 50cm deep, and each one will be a nursery for two to three thousand cherry-coloured eggs; it takes almost two months for the fertilized eggs to hatch; the optimal water temperature for the hatching is 7 or 8 degrees Celsius; and so on . . .

I learnt a great many things about salmon, and yet I didn't manage to write a single line. Without the imagination to stimulate and enliven it, plain facts are dull and inert. It was then that I happened to chance upon a photograph. It was of a submerged Boeing 747; for me, there was something faintly sad about it.

The enormous jumbo jet is more usually pic-tured soaring high above the clouds; there, with water lapping over its glinting silver fuselage, it seemed to be holding its breath. It must have been somewhere over the ocean when it was forced to make an emergency landing.

The submerged jet, the sad majesty of its fuselage, seemed to speak to me. Feeling compelled to answer, I couldn't tear my gaze from the photo. Ah, it wasn't a wrecked plane, but the firm body of a salmon, surging upwards through the river. A shoal of salmon. Hundreds of salmon in a single formation, they were forging their way upstream – upstream to lay their eggs.

How I envied the person whose camera had managed to capture this image. The salmon had been leaping and thronging right in front of her very eyes! Perhaps she'd put on diving gear and waded out into the water, wanting to get up close. If our roles had been reversed, I know I would have.

But the water-dwelling salmon fear those clumsy landlubbers who loom overhead, peering down at them from above, rather than looking them in the eye! Salmon don't like being looked down on like that. For them, even the eyes of a sympathetic naturalist hold an uncomfortable resemblance to those of a bear or fish eagle. The salmon aren't fooled, they know there's nothing innocent about this interest – why, they can practically hear the watcher smacking his lips.

And so, the only way of truly understanding salmon is to see the world through their eyes. All that's needed is a little imagination. You need to look through what's called 'the eyes of the heart', eyes that want to look beyond the visible. This desire is all you need; after that, anything is possible. Riding on waves of imagination, we travel to the very ends of the earth. The sweet, tender warmth of a long-anticipated first kiss is made sweeter by that anticipation, those long hours spent imagining the moment when the lips finally touch.

Burning in the morning sun, the orange glow that pools on the surface of the sea stretches to the far horizon.

A hundred metres up, a fish eagle casts himself through the air in wide circles. He hasn't eaten yet today, and now he's on the hunt. His keen eyes have been scanning the surface of the water for almost half an hour, but the sardines that are normally so abundant are now nowhere to be seen. The eagle's talons seem to slice through the empty air, curved like the tines of a rake. The longer this fruitless scouring goes on, the more the emptiness in his stomach gnaws at him. Nothing but the cold air whistling by his wingtips. Rage boils up in him.

The eagle is well aware that this is the time of year when the salmon ride the cold current of the Bering Sea, travelling in vast shoals. Salmon are a particularly meaty fish, and they taste light and clean, making them one of his particular favourites. The very thought of that pale flesh is enough to make his hunger intensify.

Just then, something strange appears on the edge of his vision. Whatever it is, it's extremely large, even larger than a shark, and moving rapidly southwards. A single point of clear brilliance gleams at its centre. It looks like a submarine, racing through the water with its lights on.

The eagle drops down ten metres or so, wanting a better look. He's known hulking submarines to come to the surface in these parts, and there have been times when he mistook these strange machines for salmon shoals, swooping down only to find himself brought up short. Now, he examines the sea very carefully. Normally, he would avoid flying at a low altitude – constantly having to beat his wings in order to stay aloft is irritating, and saps his strength – but not now, when he still hasn't been able to break his fast. Just as he'd thought, the strange mass is not a submarine but a shoal of salmon. Three hundred, at the very least.

The eagle decides that he ought to leave a bit of distance between himself and the shoal, so as not to attract any unwanted attention. His sharp gaze pierces the water. The salmon are maintaining an even speed of around forty kilometres an hour. At their very heart, still he sees that single, glittering point.

The eagle opens his eyes even wider and focuses on that point. It looked like a patch of clear water;

it isn't. It is a strange salmon, a kind he's never seen before. Unlike the other salmon that surround him in the shoal, the scales covering this one's back are entirely silver.

The majority of fish have pale bellies but dark blue backs. In other words, the part of them that would be visible above the water is the same colour as the sea itself; a form of camouflage, to keep them safe from prying eyes. Most of the time this is a pretty effective ruse. Many a bird has been cheated out of its supper this way.

But it isn't enough to cheat the low-flying eagle's fierce gaze, which is locked onto that oddly coloured salmon. Inside the predator's mouth, the saliva has begun to flow.

The eagle is barely two metres above the water. A delicious breakfast is now only seconds away. The eagle flexes his feet, extending his claws as far as they will go, and snatches at the water with a quick darting movement. Those claws are now embedded in the oddly coloured salmon's flesh.

'Eagle! Scatter!'

The salmon churn up the water as they flee from the aerial attack.

The eagle drives back up into the air, feeling the weight of the life flapping between his claws. Satisfied, he looks down at his catch. Clutched in his powerful feet, a salmon wriggles and writhes, desperately trying to rekindle the spark of its rapidly extinguishing life. But rather than that shining Silver Salmon being his prize, the weight of his trophy is the leaden drag of failure.

Silver Salmon had managed to avoid becoming a meal for the fierce eagle.

And yet, something strange - rather than the giddy relief of having cheated death, he feels a pang of sadness at having escaped unharmed. Because the salmon who *had* been caught - the one who'd swum by his side ever since they left their home river, who'd wordlessly passed a meal of prawns from her mouth to his, who'd even caught delicious, dragonfly-shaped insects for him, and stroked his belly with her soft fin – had been his sister.

'*Sister* . . .' Silver Salmon mouths the word to himself. His chest throbs as though scraped by a sharp rock. Just then, he hears his sister's voice, faint, filled with the rush of the water.

'*Silver Salmon* . . .' It's a memory, from about a year after they had first left the river and swum out into the sea. 'Did you know that your whole body is covered with silver scales?'

'I'm silver?' Silver Salmon was genuinely surprised.

'Every other salmon has a back the colour of dark blue seawater, but not you.' He really hadn't known about his silver scales. He'd always just assumed that his belly was white and his back was dark blue, like all the other salmon. 'Unfortunately, there's no way for us to look at ourselves.'

'Why not?'

'Well, because fish only have eyes side by side at the front of their heads, you see.'

His sister told him that the only way for salmon to get an idea of their own image is through the mouths of other salmon. Other salmon's words, she said, are mirrors that reflect you back at yourself. Perhaps this is why salmon are so fond of gossiping about each other.

'Then why do flatfish have both eyes on the same side?'

'The flatfish ended up like that because they spent so long struggling to get a look at themselves.' The thought of those ridiculous flatfish made Silver Salmon laugh. But his sister's eyes were haunted by deep shadows. 'Silver Salmon, do you know why our fellow salmon call you a different species?'

Different species. Silver Salmon had heard those words before, but only then did he seem to understand a little of what they meant. They meant that he was set apart, not one with the shoal like all the others. They made Silver Salmon think of an island lying all on its own, far out in the middle of the ocean. The loneliness of being the only thing visible above the sea that we call this world. Loneliness is more sad than frightening. Silver Salmon had many thoughts like these after discovering the truth about his peculiar colour.

'Life is unbearable!' said Silver Salmon, but it wasn't really him, it was another Silver Salmon inside him.

And then came the reply: '*But you have to bear it all the same.*' He felt divided in two.

One day, Silver Salmon made an announcement. 'Please try to look past my scales,' he said to his fellow salmon. 'I want you to look inside my heart.'

A pair who were swimming close by asked, 'How are you supposed to look inside someone's heart?'

Silver Salmon didn't notice their frowns of annoyance. He was too excited by the thought that, finally, another salmon had shown an interest in what he had to say.

'Well, I, what I mean is . . . looking inside, you know . . . past, um, external appearance . . .' His innermost feelings had suddenly become clear, he was desperate to put them into words, and yet he couldn't stop stammering. Perhaps he was simply overwhelmed. The stream of words that he could hear inside his mind came out broken and disordered. 'And inside, um – inside is something, something invisible, but . . .'

'I don't get it,' one of the pair butted in. He sounded bored. 'It's too complicated for us.' They turned their backs on Silver Salmon, hurrying off in search of food.

A couple of amused snorts came from a nearby group of salmon, who had been watching all the while. Shaking their heads, they whisper privately amongst themselves. 'He ought to be grateful for the protection he's getting,' one says, 'never mind coming out with that load of old nonsense.'

'That's right,' another chimed in, 'it'll be Silver Salmon's fault if we're the first to be attacked!'

Listening to this mockery, Silver Salmon burns with anger.

Silver Salmon had been swimming in the centre of the shoal ever since they'd begun to head south. The decision had been made by Big-Mouth Salmon, the shoal's leader. He liked to show off in front of the others and seemed incapable of lowering his voice, even when spouting the most trivial stuff imaginable. Brimming with self-confidence, he was constantly flapping his jaw, and that was how he'd got his name.

The shoal had just completed its preparations for moving off when Big-Mouth Salmon thrust himself in front, shouting, 'Don't swim too near the surface! Don't turn to look behind you! Keep your eyes peeled at all times!' Big-Mouth Salmon's word is law. 'And *you*!' He jerked his big jaw in Silver Salmon's direction. '*You* need to swim in the centre, at all times. An enemy would have no trouble picking you out from the crowd. You want to stay alive, don't you, and make it back home? Well then, you'd better make sure you do exactly as I say.'

The other salmon formed a protective wall, surrounding Silver Salmon on all sides. In front, behind, to the left and to the right, above and below, it was all salmon. But to him, this wasn't a safe fence. It was pitch-black darkness itself.

After that, Silver Salmon gradually got used to

the life of a loner. Out of all the hundreds of salmon, his sister was the only one who had a word to spare for him.

'Why are the others leaving me out?'

'What makes you think they're leaving you out? Isn't it rather that they're surrounding you, protecting you?' His sister always tried to see only the positive in every situation. It made Silver Salmon feel bad. Did she really not understand that things weren't always just as she'd like them to be? Or was she just pretending?

'But I'd rather be unprotected and have more freedom, than be protected and left out.'

'Freedom?' The word made his sister's eyes widen in shock.

The word 'freedom' is forbidden to salmon, along with words like resistance, escape, disobedience, defiance, destruction, revolution. If they used these words, Big-Mouth warned them, not a single one of them would be left alive to return to their home river and spawn.

'I want to swim freely. I want to ride the swift

currents all over the ocean, and see everything there is to be seen.'

His sister glanced around, checking to see if anyone was listening.

'Of course, I understand how you feel. But . . .' She always said she understood. 'All of this is for your own good. You must realize that's true. Only then will you grow up to be a great salmon.' Silver Salmon was so miserable he felt as though his gills would burst. 'I really worry about you.'

But of the two of them, it was his sister's attitude that Silver Salmon found disturbing. *She does nothing but worry,* he would think. *Why can't she see things from my point of view? She's trying to look down on me, just like bears and eagles do. She's only pretending to be worried so she can interfere. She doesn't understand that love is different from interfering. She doesn't know what love really is: swimming side by side, gazing silently at one another.*

Whenever these thoughts take hold of him, Silver Salmon is seized with the desire to put as much distance as possible between himself and the other salmon. *Well, why don't I?* he thinks to himself, but the other Silver Salmon inside him quickly counters: *you mustn't*. Silver Salmon couldn't count the times he'd imagined leaving the shoal, but that was only in his imagination; in reality, he could never quite get up the courage.

Perhaps it was the thought of his sister that held him back. His Sister Salmon, who'd sacrificed herself to that eagle to save him! Perhaps her final gift to him was the knowledge that he had to go on living, and in no other world but this. Until the very end.

The light is incredibly clear today.

For the past few days the sky was almost blotted out with snow, but today the sun's rays penetrate deep down into the sea. The sea's stormy indigo is ribboning out across its surface, like ink dissolving in water. After that it grows docile, a wild animal newly tamed, until there even seems something refreshing about its occasional stirring cries.

The salmon have been granted some spare time. During such times they have to build themselves up by consuming large amounts of highly nutritious food. Once they're swimming upriver, on the way to the spawning grounds, it doesn't matter how many delicious things they might see – they absolutely mustn't eat them, not then. Instead, they must store up energy reserves in advance.

Silver Salmon is quite particular when it comes to food, and he has a special soft spot for prawns. That savoury prawn taste never fails to make his mouth water. All the same, he doesn't gorge himself. It's a wise fish who doesn't let his eyes grow bigger than his belly, Silver Salmon thinks. Salmon have salmon-sized appetites, just like whales have whale-sized appetites. If salmon had whale-sized appetites . . . well, then there wouldn't even be salmon any more. A whale wouldn't be a whale if it had a salmon-sized appetite. Salmon are salmon only as long as they live a life appropriate to salmon.

Once his stomach is full, Silver Salmon cautiously pokes his head out of the water. His action causes the sea to open a window in itself, revealing a hidden part of the world. But it's also extremely dangerous. In this world, after all, the number of enemies always outweighs the number of friends.

It's been a long time since this part of the world has known such a heavy snowfall, and the ground has been transformed into an endless expanse of dazzling silver. The shoal is now in the vicinity of Alaska, a frozen realm of snow and ice. Silver Salmon can't help but be moved when he sees how the snow-covered ground mirrors the colour of his own body. Two silvers, separate yet one. Everyone feels a sense of affinity when they encounter something that reminds them of themselves. But this can also be an extremely dangerous thought; for fish, whose home is the water, the ground is the greatest enemy of all, one with which they can never be reconciled.

But Silver Salmon felt his heart swell with joy at the sight of this new world, lying beyond the boundaries of the ocean. The scent of that cold wind in his nostrils – the pure, fresh taste of air outside the water – was a delicious, dizzying sensation. *Why can't salmon live out of the water?* he asks the other Silver Salmon, the one inside him. He gets no reply. *Sometimes I think the water is a prison.* Still nothing. All of a sudden there's something there, a huge shadow swooping down over Silver Salmon's head.

'Quick,' someone screams, 'get out of the way!'

It all happens in an instant.

Silver Salmon stares about him, flinching at the smarting pain along his belly. A handful of shredded salmon scales are floating in the water, and he can scent the metallic tang of blood. He hastily twists himself this way and that, checking to see where the injury is. Strangely enough, he appears to be unharmed, though the smell of blood is gradually getting stronger. If a group of sharks picks up the scent, there will be trouble.

A gentle wave presses up against him, the sign of something closing in.

'Are you OK?' A clear, delicate voice, like a single

drop of water trembling on the tip of a fin. Another salmon. Silver Salmon calms himself down and examines the newcomer. 'Are you OK?' She is an ordinary salmon, with a pale belly and dark blue back just like all the others. But a light was sparkling in her eyes like the stars in the clear night sky.

Silver Salmon knew this because sometimes as night was falling, and without Big-Mouth Salmon knowing, he had poked his face up out of the water and watched those myriad points of light wink on, gradually lighting up the blackness. More stars, perhaps, than there were drops of water in the ocean, each boasting its own unique light, were strung together to form the Milky Way, a pale splash against the black. How did those stars seem to Silver Salmon as he gazed up with wondering eyes? Had they been the sky's own eyes, a friendly gaze looking down?

'My name is Clear-Eyed Salmon.'

While Silver Salmon had been daydreaming, she had been watching him carefully, from a distance, in case there was any danger. 'A bear swiped at you with

its big paw. You had drifted almost to the water's edge, you know. You looked as though you were lost in your own thoughts. I shouted out as soon as I saw the bear lift up its paw, and pushed you out of the way with my fin. Are you all right? You're not hurt?'

As she was anxiously asking after his health, Clear-Eyed Salmon seemed oblivious to the fact that her own dorsal fin had been ripped to shreds, and was now flapping listlessly. And wasn't that a thin trail of blood flowing from the wound? Silver Salmon groans involuntarily. Clear-Eyed Salmon had spotted the danger early, and put herself in harm's way in order to save Silver Salmon from the bear.

'Why did you do that for me? Why were you watching me in the first place?'

'I've been watching you ever since your silver scales meant you started swimming alone.'

Silver Salmon doesn't know whether he ought to feel grateful or sorry. What can you say to some-one who saved your life without even a moment's thought for their own safety? Should he tell her that he will never forget the favour? Should he offer to help her from now on, stick to her side at all times, trail her like a shadow?

Could I really give my life for another salmon? This was something that Silver Salmon had asked himself before. But different words burst out of his mouth, before he'd had time to think about them.

'You must be in terrible pain!' As soon as he'd said this he realized it didn't sound much like an expression of thanks. If only he could pick the words up and stuff them back in!

'I'm not hurt.'

'But your dorsal fin is still bleeding!'

'It's OK.'

Clear-Eyed Salmon seems to be feigning nonchalance, deliberately flicking here and there through the water as if to prove she isn't hurt. Suddenly she turns to Silver Salmon.

'If you're not hurt, then neither am I.'

'What does that mean?'

Clear-Eyed Salmon doesn't answer with words. Instead, she gazes steadily at Silver Salmon.

The light in her eyes is even more crystal clear than before. Her lips move as though mouthing words, then all of a sudden she turns and swims away, disappearing into the shoal. The scent of her trailing blood lingers in the water for some time.

Silver Salmon mulls over Clear-Eyed Salmon's words. *If you're not hurt, then neither am I.* He can't get them out of his head. Have they already made a place for themselves deep inside him, setting up a home inside his heart?

Time flows by like a river

Silver Salmon misses Clear-Eyed Salmon. Since she swam away, wounded, disappearing into the murk, there has been no opportunity for them to set eyes on each other. By the time the shoal was passing through the Bering Sea, their numbers were down to two hundred. And they have picked up the pace, too, driving forwards ever more speedily in their eagerness to arrive at the mouth of the Green River.

On days when Clear-Eyed Salmon's absence is particularly painful, Silver Salmon likes to gaze up at the stars in the night sky. The glittering stars remind him of her eyes as she looked at him, and he can't help but think that those twinkling points of light are her own way of sending him a sign, of speaking to him through them, from her heart. Saying, *I'm still here, and I'm all right.*

Silver Salmon shakes his head, disturbing the flat plane of the water's surface into a kind of gurgling laughter. He dives down as deep as he can go, hoping to drive these thoughts of Clear-Eyed Salmon from his mind, but his eyes betray him by glancing up at the stars once more.

Perhaps it's me who's sending her a sign. Perhaps that starlight shining all the way up there is our shared feelings, a secret only the two of us can know.

If that was true, then the stars were winking out an incessant refrain: *I miss you, I miss you, I miss you.* But no, Silver Salmon thinks, 'I miss you' isn't enough to do his feelings justice; for that, you would need to say something like, 'For me, there is nothing else in this world but you.' Even the decrees of Big-Mouth Salmon, the shoal's inviolable laws by which every salmon must live and die, seem as triflingly insignificant as a single drop of water when set against the vast ocean of Silver Salmon's yearning. Even the suffocating loneliness of having to swim walled around by his fellow salmon is nothing compared with the pain of not being able to see Clear-Eyed Salmon, of not sensing her there by his side.

This longing that is too great to call merely 'missing' someone, too vast to call 'waiting' for them. Life, he had felt, was unbearable, and they said he had to bear it all the same, but this eternal longing has reduced his life to a state of utter helplessness.

Silver Salmon picks up a truly odd smell, one he's sure he's never encountered before. And yet, something about it seems strangely familiar. If memories had their own scents, would this be the smell of a faint memory, of some long-ago happiness that had once suffused him? A smell embedded deep within the flesh of the mother whose face he had never known. Or was it, perhaps, the scent of his father?

A shiver of excitement ripples through the shoal.

Does this mean they have almost reached the Green River?

If it's true, if they've really made it all the way to the mouth of the Green River, then the dangers that have so far dogged them every step of the way have finally been left behind: fish eagles with their fierce glares; sharks whose cavernous mouths could swallow a whole group of salmon; polar bears that eyeballed them greedily from atop the Alaskan ice; Steller sea lions; fishing trawlers that stripped salmon from the seabed en masse, from out of every nook and cranny. If this is the mouth of the Green River . . . if it truly is the way back home, the home they've only ever heard tales of . . .

The shoal speeds up in wordless unison, fins slicing through the water. A fresh feeling wells up inside each and every salmon as the scent of the river gradually grows stronger. The shoal swings, as one, towards this thrilling, intoxicating scent. As though all this had been decided beforehand.

As the river water mingles with that of the sea, Silver Salmon notices a sharp decrease in the saltiness of the water surrounding him. According to what he's heard, the Green River isn't particularly long, so the mouth, where they are now, isn't all that far from the upper reaches. The salmon will be able to press on upstream after they've spent a short period down at the mouth, adjusting to the fresh water. All their toil and torment, all the suffering they've endured, is almost at an end. Silver Salmon feels his body grow heavy and languid as this thought flashes into his mind.

Just then, something glitters in front of his eyes, a streak of light whisking past. The intensity of the light momentarily blinds Silver Salmon, blotting out all else from his field of vision. Silver Salmon watches, rapt, as that brilliant form swims right up beside him.

'Hello?' he ventures.

The voice that answers belongs to none other than Clear-Eyed Salmon.

'Silver Salmon, how have you been? Has it been terribly difficult for you?' Silver Salmon feels his cheeks flush hot, as though he's been caught in an embarrassing predicament. 'There's no need for you to worry any more. Not now I'm here.'

A brief silence spins itself out between them. Both of them seem to be waiting for the other to make the next move, but this hesitation is making the situation increasingly awkward. Finally, Silver Salmon works up the courage to break the silence.

'Where have you been all this time?'

'Far away.'

'But where?'

'Well . . . "far away" really just means apart from you, you know. We couldn't see each other or talk to each other, so that meant there was a huge gulf between us, even though we were moving and breathing as part of the same shoal. But not any more.'

'I see what you mean, when you put it like that. Do you mind me asking you another question?'

'Please, whatever you like.'

'Just now, when you swam in front of me – what was that light? My eyes were dazzled, you see.'

'A light?'

'Yes, an intense light, blindingly bright. It was definitely there. And it was coming from you!'

A small burst of air bubbles escapes from Clear-Eyed Salmon's mouth, streaming out into the water. She seems to be laughing.

'You saw a light because you saw me with your inner eyes. The whole world appears dazzlingly beautiful when you look at it through those eyes – when you look at it with your heart.'

The eyes of the heart! Hadn't Silver Salmon heard those words before, a long, long time ago? He spent so long gazing at Clear-Eyed Salmon, this marvellous friend who knew how to see the world with the heart, that the words he had been about to say vanished completely from his mind.

This reunion with Clear-Eyed Salmon marked a huge change in Silver Salmon's life.

In the time they spent together at the mouth of the Green River, every little thing that occurred there – occurrences so trifling they barely warranted the name, to which he would have remained utterly indifferent if things had been the way they were before Clear-Eyed Salmon came back to him – was imbued with deep significance. The small, smooth form of a single pebble; a supple blade of water-weed that waved in the current; hours whose passage was broken up into discrete moments, each one saturated with the sense of the here and now; all of these things, that had seemed so trifling, had the weight and brilliance of jewels. Every single object seemed absolutely imperative for the existence of the world as a whole. And none would ever be discarded.

Silver Salmon could spend hours on end just listening out for the various sounds that travelled through the water. Before, he had only really thought of his sense of hearing as something purely practical, to help him detect food :
enemies, but during this time it became a conduit through which he was able to receive and understand the delicate shiftings of the world.

Silver Salmon listened to the insects crying in the reed beds, to a distant train rattling across an iron bridge, to the other salmon mating in preparation to swim upstream, to the rain on the surface of the sea, a sound like the mournful wail of a pipe organ, to powder-soft grains of sand sifting down through the water, to the river's deepest currents, letting each sound penetrate deep inside him.

Whatever he was listening to, Clear-Eyed Salmon was always by his side.

'You didn't realize I was here, did you?' she asked, looking at him askance.

'Of course I did! I watch you wherever you go. It's impossible for me not to know where you are.'

'Oh! You know, it's the same for me. I even know what you're hearing right now, and the kind of thoughts you're having.'

Clear-Eyed Salmon's eyes shine clear and bright. The time has come to say the words she's been keeping inside her – words that she's long been wanting to whisper to Silver Salmon, words meant for his ears only, meant for no one but him to understand, to believe.

She brought her mouth to Silver Salmon's ear, whispering so quietly that he felt rather than heard those long-unspoken words:

'I can only fall in love with a salmon whose eyes know how to see the world as beautiful.'

An inexpressible force surges up into Silver Salmon's chest, threatening to burst out from inside him. He was different from the Silver Salmon he had been before meeting Clear-Eyed Salmon. He forgot the names, appearances and characteristics of all the salmon he used to know; all the memories he had kept dissolved into nothingness, leaving an utter void within him. And this void was filled with Clear-Eyed Salmon. There was no space left for anything but her. The past was rendered entirely meaningless, not even a shadow of the gloriously meaningful present that was life with Clear-Eyed Salmon. Silver Salmon felt like a jar from which the dank, turgid water had all been sluiced out, now filled with a sharp, fresh wind.

His body, too, was changing.

Since his arrival at the mouth of the Green River – or, to be exact, since his reunion with Clear-Eyed

Salmon – a faint suggestion of reddish pink had begun to be noticeable in Silver Salmon's scales. Clear-Eyed Salmon's body, meanwhile, was undergoing an even more striking transformation, becoming gradually dappled with patches of a more intense, more orange red than those that were appearing on Silver Salmon. Instead of fading, the colour deepened as it spread across her whole body.

Autumn was deepening too.

It was around then that splashes of crimson began to be seen bobbing up and down on the surface of the river; fallen leaves, being carried out to sea.

Silver Salmon, who had known the leaves when they were young and green, asked, 'Why have you turned red?' The floating leaves drifted together, forming a mouth that could answer his question.

'Because the year is ageing,' they said. 'Because autumn is deepening.'

'Autumn?'

'That's right. We spent the rest of the year hanging from the trees, but as the days grow shorter and the year grows ripe, we have to leave.'

'Leaving must be sad, mustn't it?' Silver Salmon watches the leaves with a look of pity.

'No, it isn't sad. It's necessary. We have to go so that new leaves can hang from the trees next year. What about you salmon? Where are you heading to?'

'We're going to the upper reaches of the Green River. Going back.'

'Why?'

'Even I don't know that yet.'

'So, why have you turned red?' Just as Silver Salmon was curious about the leaves, so they too are wondering about him.

'I'm not sure about that either.'

In no time at all, the fallen leaves blanket the surface of the river, their numbers increasing to the point of being impossible to count. Enveloped within the water, the salmon swim upriver, while over their heads the leaves follow the river's course down to the open sea.

Thinking that Clear-Eyed Salmon might know

more than him, Silver Salmon asks her about their changing colour. She doesn't answer immediately but fixes Silver Salmon with a piercing gaze before, eventually, opening her mouth.

'It means we've become adults, and . . .'

'And?'

'. . . and that we've fallen in love. All salmon become red when they fall in love and get married.'

'Love? So that's it! And I thought these red blotches were some kind of disease!' Silver Salmon's laughter was bright with relief. So he'd been worrying over nothing these past few days. Although, the more he thought about it, there was something quite scary about this business of becoming an adult. The word 'responsibility' flashed through his mind, and he remembered what his dead Sister Salmon had told him once: when you become an adult, suddenly there are all these things that you have to be responsible for. Perhaps, he thought, Clear-Eyed Salmon's serious expression, which he couldn't remember seeing on her before, meant that her thoughts were running along a similar track.

'And now we are married,' Clear-Eyed Salmon said, very slowly and deliberately, 'we can have eggs.'

'Eggs?'

'Yes. Of course, there's no way you could know about it, but I already have hundreds of eggs inside me. All nestled in my belly.'

'Really? Is that true?' Silver Salmon looks startled. Fear is also written on Clear-Eyed Salmon's face, but within that fear, and in spite of it, a certain resolution already seems to be forming.

'Aren't you pleased? I need your help.' She waited for Silver Salmon to say that yes, of course he was pleased. She waited, but when no response was forthcoming she had no choice but to carry on talking herself. 'To lay the eggs, we need to swim upriver, back up to where we were born.'

Silver Salmon had been listening in silence, but at this he shook his head.

'We need to swim up there to lay the eggs? Is that the only reason?'

'It's the reason we're alive,' Clear-Eyed Salmon replied calmly.

'Stop, stop it!' Silver Salmon blurted out. He didn't want to listen to any more. Everything was getting confused inside his head.

'All salmon go through many crises, many brushes with death, in order to come this far. The shoal has to face various difficulties almost every day – that's something that will never change. But now you're telling me that the main reason we struggle so hard to stay alive, to pass through all these dangerous encounters, is just to lay eggs? That laying eggs is the only reason for two salmon to meet, and fall in love, and get married?' Silver Salmon desperately wanted for this not to be true. 'How is living solely in order to lay eggs different from living solely in order to eat? Surely no one's life can be reduced to a single reason like that. Is laying eggs the only reason that salmon swim upriver? Do you think love is just a means to an end, that laying eggs is the sum of our lives? It can't be. Salmon have a unique, specific reason for their lives, I'm sure of it. We just haven't been able to figure out what it is yet. But we have to keep trying. Otherwise, how will our lives have any meaning?'

'I can't say I agree with you. And in any case, I . . . I just have to lay eggs. But I don't mean just any eggs. I mean yours and mine.'

Clear-Eyed Salmon wanted to show Silver Salmon her pale, swollen belly. She wanted to ask him to look at their eggs with the eyes of the heart. The task of travelling to the river's upper reaches and laying her eggs; she felt a boundless pity for Silver Salmon, who was unable to grasp its importance.

'Why are the leaves floating downstream?' Silver Salmon wondered aloud. It was the Green River itself who replied: 'Because they don't know how to swim upstream.'

'What do you mean, "swim upstream"?' This ingenuous question made the Green River laugh, slackening its current. For a moment the river looked as though it had stopped flowing. But such a thing isn't possible in this world. Rivers flow on unceasingly. Still waters run deep, they say, but it's also true that the deeper the water, the more still the surface appears.

'What do you mean, "swim upstream"?' the river echoed, still chuckling to itself instead of giving an answer. 'Ah, Silver Salmon,' it said, 'you mustn't think that your own strength is enough for you to make it to the upper reaches.'

'Then what?'

'Nothing can be achieved without the help of others. Particularly not for salmon. The beauty of salmon is that they know how to swim upstream as a shoal.'

'Why do we swim upstream?'

'Swimming upstream means searching for that which isn't immediately visible. Like a dream, or hope, that is. An impossible but beautiful task.' Silver Salmon strained to catch every one of the

Green River's words, holding himself stock-still so as not to disturb the flow of understanding.

'Why do you think the water flows downstream, and you don't?' the river asked.

'Because it doesn't know how to swim upstream?'

'Ha ha ha,' the river gurgled. It shivered and shook, splashing up against its banks and making the slender stalks in the reed beds quiver. Silver Salmon finally realized that he'd been interpreting the river's words too simply.

'The river flows downstream so that salmon can swim upstream,' the Green River explained.

'So that's why we swim upstream – because of the river!' Silver Salmon felt like he was finally beginning to understand.

'That's right. The river water teaches the salmon as it flows downstream.'

'Teaches us?'

'About its currents, its temperature,' the river said slowly. 'It teaches the salmon that they have to swim upstream, but not only that – it also teaches them the *reason* for this.'

Only then did Silver Salmon nod in understanding. Through its own physical presence, its sinuous, muscular movements, the river had been transmitting a certain knowledge to the salmon's own bodies.

'You said that to swim upstream is to search for hope, right?'

'That's right.'

Silver Salmon sighed despondently. 'Then hope is nothing more than laying eggs?' he asked.

'Well . . . it might be, and it might not be.'

'But that's not a real answer!'

'Well then, Silver Salmon, what do you hope for?'

The river had put him on the spot, and Silver Salmon wasn't able to summon an immediate answer. It wasn't that he couldn't think of any one thing – rather, he had too many hopes, all crowded inside him and clamouring for attention. But there was another reason that he couldn't find the words to speak concretely about hope. Because, for Silver Salmon, hope was a far too mysterious, invisible, inexpressible thing.

The calm, deep blue of the river's body. The feeling of safety and security, of being watched over by a strong, compassionate presence. With your body immersed in those warm depths, you feel fitted into such a snug embrace that you can't tell whether or not the water is flowing past you.

'Silver Salmon, you must have seen the sea!' The Green River, whose life was lived separate from that of the sea, was insatiably curious about this much larger body of water. 'Will you tell me about it?'

'Well, for one thing, the sea has no end.' Silver Salmon felt like an old hand when it came to the sea, and could make these pronouncements with confidence.

'No end to its great breadth, you mean?'

'No, not that; it's the struggle that has no end. I'm talking about a ceaseless struggle of mutual biting and tearing and killing. That's why its waters are always rough and choppy, never calm and still like yours.'

'That's just what your father said,' the river muttered in an undertone. It seemed to be talking to itself, but Silver Salmon's sharp ears picked up the word 'father'.

'You knew my father?' he asked excitedly.

'In a sense.' This cagey answer only served to fire Silver Salmon's curiosity, and he pestered the river to tell him everything. Eventually, it gave in. 'Your father was a Silver Salmon just like you – his whole body glittered with silver scales.'

'Ah!' Silver Salmon exclaimed. His heart was racing, and he felt a lump rise into his throat. Picturing those silver scales to himself, the tears sprang to his eyes. 'And was there any other similarity? Or just the silver scales?'

'No, it's not only in your appearance that you resemble your father; your heart is just the same as his was. He was well versed in how to read the thoughts and feelings of others.' The Green River paused for a moment, dredging up memories of the past. 'Your father was the leader of the shoal. All the salmon respected him, and he in turn showed love for each and every one of them. He led around five hundred salmon back here to me. It was magnificent – a truly solemn, awe-inspiring sight. I've not yet seen another to beat it. And perhaps I never will.'

The face of the Green River flushes, as though suffused by the memory of the deep emotion that had so moved him back then. The red glow of the setting sun on the surface of the water.

'But nothing stays the same in this world. Everything is constantly changing – too quick for me.'

'What happened?'

The Green River hesitates, well aware that one should not be too reckless in raking up the past, especially when that past is filled with painful memories. But Silver Salmon needed to hear these facts from him. If he could just give Silver Salmon a few hints about what happened to his father, perhaps he, the son, might find a new reason to live.

'Your father didn't believe in taking the easy way.'

'What sort of way is that?'

'For example, something like the artificial waterway that humans have made for salmon. If you go that way, you're pretty much guaranteed to make it to the upper reaches, and without any particular dangers or difficulties. But your father was against it.'

'I'm not sure I understand.'

'Your father, he always said that for salmon, there's the salmon's way. In the past, there were many rapids in this river.'

'Rapids? What are they?'

'Well, for your father "rapids" were something which salmon absolutely have to overcome. But for those salmon who give up in the face of them and swim upriver the easy way, the way the humans made, they're nothing but frightening, impassable cliffs.'

'And something happened because of these rapids?'

'That's right. When the shoal reached the rapids, they split into two factions – your father's side, who insisted that the rapids had to be leapt over, and the opposite side, who wanted to take the easy way.'

The more he heard, the more Silver Salmon wanted to know. He pressed the river with question after question. 'Why didn't they listen to my father? After all, he was their leader.'

'They were of the opinion that leaping over the rapids was too great a sacrifice. But of course, your father thought differently. He said that, however desperately sad the sacrifice of the moment might be, it was for the sake of the distant future that they had to overcome the rapids all the same. In other words, he was worried that the more salmon grew to like taking the easy way, the more their numbers would be whittled down as years went by. Watching the other salmon as they ever-so-slowly allowed themselves to be domesticated by humans, your father realized that if things went on like this, at some point in the future there wouldn't be a single salmon left who would be both able and willing to pit itself against the rapids.'

'And what happened after that?'

Gazing sadly at the setting sun, the Green River said, 'In the process of leaping over the rapids, there were many casualties. When they arrived at the upper reaches, your father was heavily criticized by the opposite faction. And so, after apologizing on behalf of all those salmon who had been lost, he announced that he was giving up his position as leader.'

'So, that means he was at fault – he even acknowledged it himself.'

'No, Silver Salmon. Your father hadn't done anything wrong. It wasn't the rapids themselves that the dead salmon had fallen victim to, but the humans who'd hidden themselves by the side of the river, waiting to catch as many salmon as they could. They were the ones who were at fault, if anyone was. All your father did was to suggest that the salmon go the salmon's way, as was only right.'

'Ahhh.' A long sigh escapes from between Silver Salmon's lips.

The river embraces him tightly and calls him gently by his name. 'Silver Salmon . . .'

'Please,' Silver Salmon wavers, 'say what you have to say.'

'Are you sad? Do you wish I hadn't told you what I did?'

'No.'

'There, there, it's all right. You might not be the leader of your shoal but, just like your father, you have a heart that baulks at taking the easy way. I'm as proud of you as I was of him.'

This was the last time the Green River spoke to Silver Salmon of his father. Though it had been something of a sad story, hearing it had left Silver Salmon's expression imperceptibly brighter. He was no longer ashamed of his silver scales; if anything, he now considered them something to be proud of. Even when his fellow salmon teased him, calling him names like 'silver freak' and 'different species', he would simply reply with a smile, 'That's right, I'm Silver Salmon.'

Thinking back on it now, he couldn't believe he'd allowed himself to suffer so much because of something as trivial as his appearance. He remembered asking the other salmon to look inside him, at his heart, and how this had only served to confuse them and make them resent him. This world, which teaches us to focus on external appearances when we should be able to see each other heart-to-heart, seemed filled with hypocrisy.

Little by little, though, Silver Salmon began to realize that he'd been arrogant.

'I've been demanding that the other salmon look at my heart,' he said to himself, 'but have I myself really been taking a proper look at theirs?' And the other Silver Salmon, the salmon inside him, answered, '*No.*'

So. When it came down to it, he was no better than the rest. And then there was the heart of Clear-Eyed Salmon, whose only reason for living was to go to the river's upper reaches and spawn. Silver Salmon hadn't even been able to look properly at those eggs, those countless hearts which Clear-Eyed Salmon was sheltering within her. Is it, perhaps, that the closer something is to us, the harder it is to see?

These thoughts tormented Silver Salmon. The Green River was filled with pity for his suffering friend, and when it all got too much would embrace him without hesitation and let him know that he wasn't alone.

'Why do you want to go to the sea?'

The river feigned innocence. 'Me, want to go to the sea? I don't know what you mean.'

'Come on, tell the truth. Why, even now you're flowing downstream, never content to just stay where you are!'

'Well, I suppose that's true. But there's no reason for me to go to the sea.'

Silver Salmon hadn't realized that the river had this faintly absurd side to him.

'A life without a reason – is such a thing really possible?'

'Certainly not according to you.'

'Then what's the reason for your life?'

'The reason for my life is that I exist, right here, right now – that in itself.'

'Existing is a reason for living?'

'That's right. Existing means being a kind of background, for things that aren't me.'

This word 'background' couldn't help but grate on Silver Salmon's ear, because it always made him think of those salmon who would use a similar word to put on airs, saying, 'I've got Big-Mouth Salmon to back me up.' They would steal others' food at the slightest provocation, and spent so much time boasting you'd think they would run out of air. They used to act as though they were laws unto themselves, albeit small fry when compared to Big-Mouth Salmon. And so the word 'background' always made Silver Salmon think of something dark and frightening.

'What is a background?'

'My surrounding you right here and now, this "presence" I make, is your background.'

'Aha!' Silver Salmon hadn't realized that the same word could have such a different meaning or feeling depending on who used it.

It was the same with the word 'wound'. The wound in Clear-Eyed Salmon's dorsal fin still hadn't healed, a constant reminder of the polar bear's attack. Her fin was in tatters, like a scrap of torn cloth. The other salmon were always saying it was ugly and averting their eyes so they wouldn't have to look at it. To them, a 'wound' was nothing but a scar they didn't like to look at. But to Silver Salmon that wound was his own, deep inside him. Only, he couldn't say, 'I'll shrug off my own hurt and concentrate on yours.'

'Do you get the idea now?'

'I think so. You mean that the stars shine because they have the darkness as their background?'

'Exactly.'

'Then, is it also true that the beauty of the shoal can be a background for each individual salmon?'

'That's right, yes, something like that.'

The river marvelled over Silver Salmon. Here was a salmon who thought deeply and clearly, who took an interest not only in the water, his natural element, but also in the principles of the sky and land. Understanding the beauty and laws of nature was only possible when you saw yourself as an inextricable part of nature as a whole. It was only humans, who see themselves as set apart from nature, at which they look down their noses, who remain ignorant of this fundamental truth. This was something that caused the river no end of agitation.

'Then could I be someone else's background?'

'You?'

'Why not? Do you think I'm too small?'

'No.'

'Then why did you seem so surprised?'

'Because it's such an admirable thing, to want to be someone else's background. It isn't only for those who are big, you know. Anyone can be a background for someone else.'

Silver Salmon was holding something back – that, more than anything else, he wanted to be a background for Clear-Eyed Salmon.

Silver Salmon was soon shocked to learn that he hadn't been the only one talking things over with the Green River; Clear-Eyed Salmon had also been seeking its advice, conversing with the eyes of the heart. She'd also picked up on something that Silver Salmon hadn't – the Green River was in pain.

'Where does it hurt?' she asked with a frown.

'Ah, it's not so bad . . .'

Immersed in the Green River, Clear-Eyed Salmon had detected a faint moaning. The river had been in pain all this time, but had been hiding it so that the salmon wouldn't worry. Clear-Eyed Salmon had been aware of this from the moment she swam into its waters, and especially when her eyes had grown red and swollen. Such was her empathy with those around her, their pain was mirrored in her own body.

'Show me where it hurts.' Her peremptory manner showed no trace of any embarrassment.

'The thing is – everywhere hurts. My windpipe, my veins . . .'

Clear-Eyed Salmon opened her eyes even wider, staring into the surrounding water.

'You're saying the individual droplets of water inside you make up a windpipe and blood vessels?'

'That's right. And my whole body hurts. There are times when my blood doesn't circulate properly and it's difficult to breathe.'

Indeed, the river had been increasingly short of breath the further up they went. Silver Salmon had simply assumed that he was getting worn out with all the sharp twists and turns he was making, but now it seemed there was something else going on.

'It's the sound of the trees being cut down beside me. I mean, it's not as though that didn't happen in the past too, but that was only with axes, and life was still worth living. But now, those constantly whirring power saws are so deafening I can't sleep.' He gave a deep sigh. 'It seems like every day there's something new I can't cope with. They say there will soon be a time when colourless, scentless water will gush out somehow in the humans' villages. I must be getting old.'

'Then it's humans that have made you ill!' Clear-Eyed Salmon almost shouted.

'Well . . . do you hate humans?'

'It's not about hating. It's just that I can't trust them. They don't look at us from our level, you see, they only peer down on us from above. I can't forgive them for that.'

Green River looked into Clear-Eyed Salmon's eyes, his gaze deep and profound.

'Have you ever actually seen a human?' he asked.

'I've seen hundreds of salmon caught in a net from a salmon-catcher's boat. Perhaps in the future there won't even be any salmon left for them to catch, if they keep on terrorizing us in this senseless way.'

'What I think,' the Green River said, 'is that there are two types of human: those who carry fishing rods, and those who carry cameras.'

'What's a camera?'

'You could call it a machine for capturing time.'

'Oh,' Clear-Eyed Salmon exclaimed, 'this is getting too complicated for me!'

'That's because you've never seen a human with a camera. Those are the kind of human I trust. They're a part of nature too, you see.'

That strange-sounding word, 'camera', left Clear-Eyed Salmon terribly confused. The only things she'd ever heard of humans carrying were fishing rods and nets, so she couldn't understand what the river was trying to tell her. Humans carrying cameras, what on earth was that supposed to show? Humans were humans, surely. How could the Green River trust them?

As they swam upstream, the salmon flushed a progressively deeper red, and their lips began to bulge out. The male salmon's teeth grew long and sharp, poking out between their lips so their mouths looked to be bristling with razors. This change happened because they had fallen in love, and needed to protect their female from any enemies.

Silver Salmon came across a salmon with a severely crooked back. His deformity was obvious when compared with other male salmon, the kink in his spine making it look as though he was permanently on the verge of making a sharp turn to the left. It was especially apparent whenever he stopped swimming and held himself still for a while.

When he encountered this odd-looking Bent-Back Salmon, Silver Salmon was the first to speak.

'Hello!' No answer. 'What happened to your back?' Still no answer. 'Can't you open your mouth?' Silver Salmon shouted, exasperated. But Bent-Back Salmon still showed no sign of having heard. The only thing that betrays any possible response is the minute trembling of one fin, which seemed to spasm.

Now the penny dropped: in addition to having a crooked back, Bent-Back Salmon was mute. Only then did Silver Salmon realize that the excessive interest he'd been showing in the other salmon's appearance was likely to be making him feel terribly ashamed.

Instead of using words, Silver Salmon spoke from the heart: 'I'm sorry.'

'It's OK,' Bent-Back Salmon replied in the same way, and with equal feeling. He explained that he'd never been sure why he looked the way he did.

'Perhaps it's because of the colourless, scentless water that flows out of the humans' village,' Silver Salmon suggested.

A pained expression flitted over Bent-Back Salmon's face as he swam awkwardly alongside.

Suddenly the current grew stronger, churning up the water into a rough, tempestuous maelstrom. If you didn't hold yourself strongly, the sheer force of the current would instantly sweep you down-river. The experience reminded Silver Salmon of the time the shoal had encountered a tidal wave, far out in the open ocean. He glanced around at the other salmon to see how they were faring; most looked to be engaged in a fierce battle to retain control of the line of their body.

The roar of the water seemed as though it would swallow the entire shoal in a single gulp, sucking

them into its maw. Whatever was causing this terrible din was directly in front of them, from which direction countless air bubbles were scattering and gathering, gathering and scattering. Silver Salmon furled his fins and steeled himself, flexing every muscle in his body. Just then, someone up ahead shouted, 'Rapids!'

At this, the other salmon all stopped in their tracks.

Though he had, of course, heard the word, Silver Salmon had no idea what these rapids actually looked like. And he was never one to stifle his own curiosity.

He thrust his way up through the water, poking his head up and breaking the surface. Just as the sea had always done, the river opened a window in its chest and revealed the world to him.

Rain was pouring down from the sky in thick ropes, battering the river's surface. As though it had been waiting for a witness, a brilliant rainbow begins to spread its iridescent colours through the sky, all in front of Silver Salmon's wondering eyes. The rainbow truly is the most wondrous of all the sights these eyes have ever seen. What with the myriad raindrops pelting down and churning up the surface, Silver Salmon wasn't able to feast his eyes on that mysterious rainbow for anywhere near as long as he would have liked. He was afraid of being lashed by the rain's cruel whips and sent spinning away downriver, and this fear drove him back underwater.

Silver Salmon couldn't wait to tell Clear-Eyed Salmon all about the rapids he'd seen, and try, though it had all happened in an instant, to explain something of the mystery and wonder of the rainbow that had captured his gaze. His thoughts were wandering far away from the matter at hand.

'I saw a rainbow, a rainbow!'

'That's nice.' For whatever reason, Clear-Eyed Salmon seemed much less enthused than Silver Salmon had expected.

'Did you see it too?'

'No.'

'Don't you want to?'

'Not particularly.' Clear-Eyed Salmon rolled her

eyes, seemingly baffled by Silver Salmon's excitement. 'Rainbows only ever exist for a brief moment. They disappear almost straight away.'

'And therefore they're not beautiful, you mean?'

'Perhaps.'

Clear-Eyed Salmon took a long, steady look at Silver Salmon. For her, there is an air of greatness about him, he who knows how to look beyond the here and now and imagine the various turns their lives might take at some point in the future. More than anything else, she loves him. And yet, he still doesn't seem to have fully grasped just how perilous a place this world is. That's why he can come out with what are, to her, such ridiculously wrong-headed statements as 'laying eggs is not enough of a reason for living'.

'There was a salmon, once, who said that having hope meant wanting to catch hold of a rainbow, and that chasing rainbows was the reason for living. Waking or sleeping, it was all he ever did. He even left the shoal and struck out on his own, promising to return once he'd caught a rainbow.'

'And did he? Catch one, I mean?'

'He kept on seeing rainbows, and not just in the sky – he even saw them when whales sprayed water out of their blowholes. The more rainbows he saw, the stronger his desire to catch one grew. It was all-consuming. But in the end, he couldn't succeed.'

'Why not?'

'That's the nature of rainbows; if you catch them, they disappear. They say that in the end, a mere two days after he abandoned the shoal, the salmon died. Floating belly-up on the surface of the sea, with the whites of his eyes visible.' The image made Silver Salmon shudder. 'There's such a thing as an iron window, they say. When humans hold it up and the sunlight glances off it at a particular angle, it makes a glittering rainbow. That salmon, the one who died, also saw that kind of rainbow. As it was much nearer to hand than the sky's rainbow or the whale's rainbow he threw caution to the wind and flung himself at it immediately, imagining an easy end to his quest. He'd be back with the shoal in no time at all, he thought, showing off his prize – but instead, he ended up impaled on the iron window.'

Before she knew it, Clear-Eyed Salmon's eyes had filled with tears. Each tear held a message for Silver Salmon, one she was desperate to convey: that chasing rainbows was ultimately and utterly futile.

'Something doesn't have to be far off to be beautiful. It doesn't have to be on such a grand scale, either. And it doesn't need to vanish in the space of a moment.'

The roar of the water as it crashes down over the rapids was getting louder and louder. The rapids have halted the shoal's smooth progress, and the salmon felt cowed and unsettled by all the noise and confusion. Silver Salmon began to regret his boasting about having seen the rainbow. In all respects, Clear-Eyed Salmon was certainly the more mature of the pair. Silver Salmon made a firm resolution to protect her, to safeguard a love that would endure long after the rainbow's fleeting beauty.

As luck would have it, they were told that a full-shoal conference had just been called, so there was no more time just then for idle fantasies about rainbows.

It was the first such conference to be held since they'd arrived at the Green River. Big-Mouth Salmon swam to the head of the shoal, tracked by the collective gaze of the salmon. The expression on his face was stern.

'Let us freely discuss how we propose to pass through these rapids we see before us.' This was a much more courteous tone than they were used to hearing from him – was that really Big-Mouth Salmon talking? And was it possible that he was also trembling? It was almost imperceptible, but yes, the pectoral fin next to his gills was shaking. So the impassable cliff known as the rapids had cowed even Big-Mouth Salmon. Perhaps this sudden weakness he was now displaying had been there all along, and ruling over the shoal with all his bluff and bluster had seemed the best way of concealing it, just as the fretful way in which young salmon are always pestering their elders stems from the knowledge of their own weakness.

When Big-Mouth Salmon moved aside, Bag-of-Bones Salmon was first to be given the floor. Unlike the other salmon, who devoted themselves whole-heartedly to finding food, he spent all of his time conducting academic research, his ascetic lifestyle visible in his emaciated frame. As a scientist, he sees his task as to improve the stages in the lives of salmon, and yet he doesn't even have the wits to take care of his own health. But this didn't bother Bag-of-Bones Salmon in the slightest – his self-conceit was too entrenched for anything to dent it.

'I have ascertained,' he said, 'that the rapids currently blocking our path are precisely 10 metres in width and 3 metres in depth.' This was Bag-of-Bones Salmon all over: finicky to a fault.

'Ah!' This single exclamation escaped from the myriad mouths that made up the shoal. The scientist indicates the direction of the rapids, from which the water's muffled roar is still coming, with a nonchalant flick of his eyes.

'Four years ago, when we were nothing but tiny

salmon fry, we each of us leapt down these selfsame rapids. At that time, we were 6,367,941 in number. Of those, 1,512,832 made it from the river to the sea, and this year ten shoals, comprising a total of 3,265 salmon, have returned, here to the Green River. We must not forget the fact that we ourselves are one of these shoals.'

Bag-of-Bones Salmon was also in possession of an exceptional memory. His mind was like an enormous storehouse where all manner of facts are filed and preserved. Circling over the riverbed, he mutters to himself, 'Yes, the rapids have increased in height by 35 centimetres since we leapt down over them.'

Suddenly everyone seemed to be talking at once. 'All right,' was the general consensus, 'we've had the numbers, now let's get down to business. How are we going to get over these rapids?'

Bag-of-Bones Salmon had his answer ready.

'By swimming at a faster speed than that of the water which is coming down over the rapids.'

'Well, but how?'

'You have to concentrate all your energy in your caudal fin.' By way of demonstration, the scientist waved his own poor excuse for a fin at them. 'If, for the sake of argument, we take the velocity of the falls to be 30 kilometres per hour, that means we would have to produce speeds in excess of 40 kilometres per hour. At least.'

'And what's the *actual* velocity of the falls?'

'That is precisely the issue upon which I am aiming to shed some light with my current research.' There was a loud groan of disappointment.

'Well, a fat lot of good that is, then!'

'My research merely aims to develop a theory,' Bag-of-Bones Salmon said tetchily. 'There's no way for me to be any more specific than that.'

'You're going to have to get up over those rapids too, no?'

'Naturally.'

'Do you know how?'

'Not yet. I'll, ah, I'll just go and investigate that now.' The scientist beat a hasty retreat from the conference, swimming away under the dark rocks. His retreating figure looks especially lonely as he vanishes into the gloom.

The second to take the floor was Smooth-Tongued Salmon.

He had what is called the gift of the gab; no other salmon could touch him when it came to holding forth with eloquence. His rhetoric was always impeccably deployed, his enunciation was crystal clear, and his delivery couldn't be faulted.

Swimming up to the head of the shoal, he complained that the spot Big-Mouth Salmon and Bag-of-Bones Salmon had spoken from was too cramped for delivering a proper speech. And besides, he, Smooth-Tongued Salmon, was used to speaking from an elevated place so he could look down over his audience. Couldn't they raise the rostrum? As the other salmon were eager to hear what the orator had to say, they quickly made a space for him on the highest stone.

But still he wasn't satisfied.

'I need a lectern too.'

'What for?'

'For when I get to a really stirring bit and need something to strike my caudal fin on. For emphasis, you know. It's an established oratorical technique.'

A couple of salmon pushed a flat stone over and placed it in front of Smooth-Tongued Salmon. The shoal strain forwards as one, eagerly anticipating what he's going to come out with. No one does 'sincere and impassioned' quite like Smooth-Tongued Salmon.

'Ladies and gentlemen present here!' His resonant syllables are audible even over the roar of the water as it crashes down over the rapids. 'We stand here today facing a great trial, the outcome of which is as yet unknown. The name of this trial? You've heard it already: the rapids. This trial is one which nature itself has set out for us, one which will ultimately determine our individual success or failure in life.' The salmon in the audience had started to bow their heads practically as soon as the oration began. Something about those flowing, declamatory clauses always has a soporific effect. 'I say to you all, if we combine our strength . . .' Those with their heads lowered have started to doze off, but Smooth-Tongued Salmon pays no heed, continuing to work himself up into the kind of passion necessary for great speech-making. 'I say to you all, if we combine our intelligence . . . I say to you all, we must band together, and yet more firmly together, as one . . .'

How much time had passed?

Waking sluggishly from his doze, Silver Salmon sees that Smooth-Tongued Salmon has gone red in the face, trying to regulate his breathing so that he can recite the final part of his speech with the maximum intensity: '. . . I say to you all, to all of you salmon, I cry out for your hearts to melt in warmth and love!'

'Wow!'

As though they'd planned it this way, no sooner had Smooth-Tongued Salmon finished his speech than the very salmon who'd slept through the whole thing sent up a chorus of rousing cheers. Perhaps they're cheering because they're relieved that the pointless speech has finally come to an end. The orator accepts this applause with a courteous bow and leaves the stand, satisfied that he has delivered everything he wanted to say in a manner befitting his own considerable reputation. But the salmon who were listening have been left every bit as unsatisfied as they were by Bag-of-Bones Salmon's pedantry.

'If I was applauded like that,' Silver Salmon muttered, 'I'd be so embarrassed I'd have to go and find somewhere to hide.'

Clear-Eyed Salmon put her head to one side and said, 'He doesn't seem to realize that there are times when you need to lower your voice.'

Third to take the floor was Long-Whiskered Salmon.

His task in the shoal was that of education, and all the salmon referred to him respectfully as 'teacher'. While they were still out at sea, Long-Whiskered Salmon had instilled a great many facts into the minds of the other salmon. There seemed to be nothing he didn't know. His lessons generally took this format:

'The name of our great leader?'

'Big! Mouth! Salmon!'

'Principal distribution area of salmon?'

'North Pacific and North Atlantic coast.'

'One example of a fish which also returns to the river of its birth to breed?'

'Ayu – sweetfish, from the Korean seas.'

'The reason that salmon are the lords of all creation?'

'Because we are sentient beings.'

Long-Whiskered Salmon, too, held the firm belief that it wasn't enough for salmon to merely learn about themselves – they also needed a rigorous education in the ways of humans. He never tired of stressing that, since humans are the greatest enemies of salmon, it was only by knowing as much as possible about them that the salmon would be able to triumph against their evil ways.

'The year humans first landed on the moon?'

'1969.'

'The places lauded as three great cities of beauty?'

'Sydney in Australia, Naples in Italy, Rio de Janeiro in Brazil.'

His knowledge on these matters was seemingly bottomless, and his lessons could well have gone on forever. This won him the respect of a great many of the salmon, and everyone took care to use humble language when addressing him. The other salmon were convinced that Long-Whiskered Salmon's wisdom would show them the way to overcome the cliff-like rapids.

'The thing about life,' the sage teacher explained,

'is that it's all one continuous test. And the only way to secure the future is to be prudent in the way that we approach these tests. That's all these rapids are: a test that nature has laid out to challenge us. There's an old saying: if at first you don't succeed, try, try again. So even if we fail the first time, we have to take up the challenge a second time, a third time, even a fourth time.'

'But we know all that already, teacher. We know we have to accept this challenge. What we want you to tell us is *how.*'

The one who'd had the presumption to interrupt the teacher in full flow was none other than Silver Salmon. Unused to being treated in such a way, Long-Whiskered Salmon blinked in surprise and stopped speaking for a few moments, but quickly recovered his train of thought.

'Weak, lazy salmon are stragglers, failures. Your success depends on you yourself. Everybody, take a look at Bent-Back Salmon over there. There's an example of a salmon who failed to look after himself properly.'

'Teacher!' Silver Salmon protested loudly, but Long-Whiskered Salmon seemed not to hear him, perhaps because of the general hubbub being caused by the other salmon.

'You must all strive to avoid becoming like Bent-Back Salmon.'

'Teacher, how can you say . . .' Silver Salmon had turned bright red in indignation. 'Bent-Back Salmon's disability hasn't come about because of some lack of effort on his part. It's the humans' bad water, which they spill into the rivers and seas, that's made him the way he is. His bent back causes him terrible suffering. But there's something that pains him even more than the agony of not being able to swim properly. Have you ever thought about what that might be? It's the pain of wanting to help others, but simply not being able to. That's what's hurting Bent-Back Salmon.'

Still, Long-Whiskered Salmon refused to back down. 'I wasn't intending to shame him,' he said loftily. 'I was simply using him as an example.'

Silver Salmon couldn't listen to any more of this.

These words seemed to him nothing but a poor attempt to excuse bad behaviour.

'The teacher seems to think that lessons are the be-all and end-all of life. Perhaps, even while watching the fallen leaves floating on the river's surface, he's thinking about the morals that could be drawn from it. If he were to come across a flower he hadn't seen before, rather than marvelling at its beauty, he would bury his head in an illustrated guide to plants, wanting to know only whether there was some practical benefit to be had from the flower. Even when he gazes up at the stars, perhaps he's searching for a lesson there. He doesn't understand that flowers and stars are beautiful in themselves. Even with his painfully crooked back, Bent-Back Salmon does the best he can. But the teacher can't understand why his pain is beautiful, why his disability is beautiful. Because the teacher can only teach.'

Fourth up to the front is Seer Salmon.

He is a soothsayer, the one who chooses each salmon's name when it is born, and predicts the fate that will befall them in the days to come. His fame grew after he predicted that Big-Mouth Salmon would become the leader of the shoal, and it was widely known that, whenever there was some difficulty that needed solving, Big-Mouth Salmon would come to him for advice. Though Seer Salmon had taken upon himself the task of choosing names for the other salmon, he hadn't, of course, been able to choose one for himself. The other salmon thought this was something of a shame, and had themselves given him the name Seer Salmon.

As Seer Salmon swam up to the front, he looked deep into the eyes of each salmon he passed, one by one. His face was always eerily blank, entirely free from the tensions and concerns that frequently plagued the other salmon.

'It is the wrath of heaven that has sent this fierce water of suffering to us!'

Seer Salmon claimed to have the ability to communicate with the heavens whenever he chose. The majority of the salmon weren't quite so credulous as to take that at face value, but all the same, there were a decent number who said, 'In any case, it would be good if it was true. I don't see any harm in it; why not believe what he says?'

Big-Mouth Salmon was one of these latter. He had his gaze glued to the soothsayer, straining to catch every word.

'It's perfectly evident that we can surmount these rapids. We just need a little time.' At this, the faces of the listening salmon brightened like sunshine after rain. Someone called out, 'How long should we wait?'

'Even I don't know that.'

'But you can predict the future!'

'Of course, I'm aware of our ultimate fate. But as for the precise way this fate will pan out – only the heavens know that. Only there do they have the power to decide when the time has come for us to overcome these rapids. Before that, any attempt is doomed to end in failure, however much we exert ourselves.'

The eager, hopeful expression that had been visible on Big-Mouth Salmon's face contorted into angry disappointment.

'The time for us to spawn is getting nearer every day, and it's my responsibility to guide the shoal to the spawning grounds. And you're saying we should just wait indefinitely, with no concrete plan?'

Big-Mouth Salmon abandoned the courteous language he'd used at the start of the conference. His words were blunt and to the point. But it seemed that nothing could disturb the soothsayer's preternatural calm.

'If that is the will of heaven.' Seer Salmon slowly closes his eyes.

All eyes are on Big-Mouth Salmon, on the large air bubbles popping out from between his lips at irregular intervals. His ragged breathing is clearly a sign of inner turmoil.

Just as the outcome of the conference seemed to have been left up in the air, someone shouldered their way into the circle, shouting, 'I've found the way! I said my research would be necessary to find it, and now I have!'

It was Bag-of-Bones Salmon. In an instant, all eyes were on the scientist.

'I measured every nook and cranny beneath the rapids,' he boasted. 'And at the far right-hand side I discovered a newly made passage, a kind of dark tunnel. I ascertained that the speed of the water flowing there wasn't even 10 kilometres per hour. It seems like something humans have made for us.'

'Humans?'

'Inside the dark tunnel there's a flight of steps. Each step is around 30 centimetres in height; that kind of regularity doesn't exist in nature. Only humans could have made it.'

Humans are the greatest enemies of salmon. And those selfsame humans had made a way for salmon to use! The audience couldn't believe what they were hearing.

Long-Whiskered Salmon looked particularly sceptical.

'There are countless humans who do cruel things simply in order to show that they can,' he said. 'Why is the earth a den of thieves? Why are murders committed there every day? Humans are more cruel than we salmon can imagine. How could we ever trust those who invented war?'

Several salmon nodded in agreement, chiming in with their own opinions.

'Perhaps that tunnel is a trap the humans made to lure us in.'

'It's a route to death!'

'Perhaps it's better to just die here rather than be killed by humans.'

'It's not a trap,' Bag-of-Bones Salmon insisted, 'it's a way through. I mean, I myself went right through to the end, and now here I am back again – how would I have been able to do that if it was a trap? And there isn't a scratch on me. My own body proves what I'm saying.'

Bag-of-Bones Salmon thrashed from side to side in his eagerness to show the other salmon that he'd returned unharmed – he almost looked as though he was trying to escape from a net. His emaciated body didn't seem able to take the strain. Silver Salmon, who had been listening quietly the whole while, said to Clear-Eyed Salmon, 'I think what he's saying might be true.'

'I think so too.'

'Up until now, the professor's weak point has been relying on numbers to prove the results of his research. We salmon aren't known to have good heads for figures – that meant his research was pretty much useless for us. But things are different now. Instead of relying on statistics and abstract theories, he put his own safety at risk by venturing into that dark tunnel alone. Now he has physical evidence to back up his claims.'

Silver Salmon and Clear-Eyed Salmon waved their pectoral fins in agreement.

All the energy has fizzled out from Bag-of-Bones Salmon's eyes; perhaps his recent exertions have proved too much. The other salmon form a circle around him, watching in silence as the flame of his life gutters out. His final words are little more than muttered gasps.

'The way . . . I discovered . . . is clearly . . . the easy way . . .' Those were the last words to ever pass his lips. He had spent his final breath in teaching the salmon the easy way.

His soul has departed his body, but now this body has found a new purpose for itself. It will become food for the many varieties of microorganism that live in the water, and those microorganisms will, in turn, be eaten by the next generation of baby salmon, helping them to grow up big and strong. The shoal watch in silence as Bag-of-Bones Salmon's body is carried away by the current. Humans like to make a grave for a dead person, and set up a tombstone there. For the salmon, the great size of this stone is a clear indication of the size of the vain ambitions which that human had harboured during their life. Worse than that, humans even go so far in their folly as to erect tombstones for those who are still living. Salmon, on the other hand, need no monument to their dead. They prefer to look death in the face, in silence; to feel sad for the brief amount of time that is appropriate, but then to quell this sadness and move on with their lives.

'Right, let's hurry up and stop dawdling.'

Several salmon had already left their places, though the conference hadn't yet been brought to an official close. Big-Mouth Salmon was plainly at a loss. Having originally been extremely sceptical, it seemed as though he still wasn't too keen on taking the way Bag-of-Bones Salmon had found.

Now Silver Salmon swam up to the front. 'Shouldn't we think it over a little more?'

Those who had been making to leave shouted back, 'What's the use of thinking? Let's hurry up and get on with it!'

'I don't think it's right to take the easy way,' said Silver Salmon. He spoke clearly and with feeling, and the other salmon began to pay attention. 'I think that salmon should take the salmon's way.'

'What does that mean?'

Thoughts of his father had crept up on Silver Salmon unawares, and now came crowding in. His father as he imagined he must have looked as he prepared to lead the five hundred-strong shoal through the rapids. His father, a great salmon, who was never one to take the easy way.

'The easy way that humans made isn't the salmon's way.'

Salmon are naturally quick-tempered, and this piqued them.

'Don't give yourself airs!'

'What on earth have you got against this easy way?'

'I respect the departed professor, Bag-of-Bones Salmon, who discovered this easy way. And I acknowledge that he sacrificed himself trying to help us,' replied Silver Salmon. 'But we salmon have the ability to overcome the rapids ourselves! We can't just give in without even trying.'

'Don't you know what suffering that would involve?'

'Of course.'

'And we really need to put ourselves through that? We have to get to the upper reaches quickly to spawn. Time is pressing.' Clear-Eyed Salmon glances sharply at Silver Salmon, extremely curious to hear his answer.

It seems an effort for Silver Salmon to speak, but when he does he says, 'Laying eggs is extremely important.'

Clear-Eyed Salmon is shocked to hear those words come out of Silver Salmon's mouth. It's certainly the first time she's ever heard him express such an opinion. Hadn't he told her before that there's more to life than laying eggs, that finding a 'higher reason' was more important than anything else? Clear-Eyed Salmon keeps staring at Silver Salmon, her eyes shining with tears. The sight of his blushed-pink scales has never seemed so brilliant to her as it does right then.

'It's fair to say,' Silver Salmon resumes, 'that not a single one of us, when faced with the option of taking the easy way, really *wants* to try and leap up those perilous rapids.'

'He's finally come to his senses!' another salmon exclaimed sarcastically.

'But . . .' Silver Salmon pauses. Now he sees his own image overlaying that of his father. The jolt it gives him makes it difficult for him to control himself. In his mind, he sees an otherwise invisible thread connecting his father and himself. That thread is like the living, moving water, like the river's blue-tinged sighs. Having never seen the other salmon's face, there is no way for Silver Salmon to know how closely he resembles his awe-inspiring silver father from days gone by.

'I know that laying eggs is important for us salmon. But I don't think the issue is simply one of laying eggs or not – what's really important, surely, is that the eggs we lay are good and healthy. If we start by taking the easy way then our children will naturally want to follow in our footsteps, and soon it will be the only way they know. But if we leap up over the rapids, then our legacy will instead be all the suffering and joy of that single moment, the fear and exhilaration of putting everything at risk. All the actions of our lives, the choices we make and the challenges we accept, will go to make the bones and flesh of our children, becoming the substance of those future lives. And that's why we mustn't take the easy way.'

This was a very different Silver Salmon to the one who had once been so weak and ashamed. Rather than thundering out his words like Smooth-Tongued Salmon, they passed in a mere murmur from his heart to those of the salmon who were listening.

'He's right. The easy way is no way at all.'

'I think there's something beautiful in choosing not to take the easy way.'

'I'm going to do as Silver Salmon suggests.'

'I'm going to leap over the rapids too.'

The shoal gathers at the foot of the rapids. Even those who had initially suggested taking the easy way now swim towards Silver Salmon, somewhat shamefaced.

There was no need for any further discussion. It was left to Big-Mouth Salmon to sum up:

'What Silver Salmon says is right. All those who can should try to leap over the rapids. The others, like Bent-Back Salmon and those who are heavy with eggs, should take the easy way through the tunnel.'

Silver Salmon was worried about Clear-Eyed Salmon. Though she herself was one of those who were heavy with eggs, she was adamant that she would risk the rapids.

'Don't you need to lay eggs?'

'Every word you said has stuck with me. "The easy way is no way at all", you said. If you want to know the full joy of swimming upstream, then you have to be willing to have a wound torn in you – that's what I think. And that's something I want to teach the eggs in my belly.'

Hearing these stubborn words, Silver Salmon knew there was no way he would get her to yield.

Eventually they decide in what order to leap over the rapids, and while they wait for their turn Silver Salmon tells Clear-Eyed Salmon that he has a pain in his chest.

'Mine too. It's as though something keeps stabbing me.'

'Perhaps it means we're leaving something of ourselves in each other's hearts.'

'What do you mean?'

'Something to prove that we lived, and loved each other. Something that will always remain, no matter what else is lost.'

Their turn to leap is approaching.

They hear a loud splash; one of the salmon ahead of them in the queue has failed in his leap and fallen back down. Now he has to turn around and go to the back of the queue, and wait for his turn to come again. However many times it takes.

'Silver Salmon . . . did you find the meaning of life?'

'Yes, I think so. Life . . .' But there's no time for Silver Salmon to answer; his and Clear-Eyed Salmon's turn to attempt the rapids has finally come.

'Courage!' Clear-Eyed Salmon says. The pressure of the water pouring off the rapids prevents Silver Salmon from opening his eyes properly. Though he hasn't eaten anything since swimming up from the mouth of the Green River, there is still energy left in his body. He'll have to expend at least half of that energy now if he is to overcome the rapids. He has to move his caudal fin from side to side, quicker than at any other time in his life, if he is to generate the necessary speed. He has to leap with his whole body, with his whole heart.

Silver Salmon and Clear-Eyed Salmon drive up through the water with all their might. They see and hear nothing, and their minds are entirely empty of any thoughts. They are nothing but sleek, muscular

bodies leaping up over the rapids, darting through the choppy current and shooting up into the air.

What happened next was nothing short of miraculous.

Almost before they knew it, the violent ropes of water that had been pouring over the rapids were gone, and in their place was a calm, gentle current, cradling them in its soft embrace. But this was no miracle; it was reality. They really had leapt all the way over the rapids. The gravel on the riverbed sparkled iridescent in the sunlight, the tiny pebbles clinking together as the soft current swept over them. Both in front and behind are other salmon who have successfully conquered the rapids, with more joining them at every moment. That difficult, important challenge was as easy as this? They shook their heads in wonder.

Silver Salmon wanted to see the outside world. If he suggested it, he would have to wait for the river to open a window in its chest. Just this once, Silver Salmon wanted to try making a window in the river by himself, without any help.

'Perhaps, in order to do that, I need to first open a window in myself. I've been closed all this time, I see that now – I've lived my life in ignorance of anything outside myself.'

He suggested to Clear-Eyed Salmon that they poke their heads out of the water, and together they made a window in the now gentle river's chest.

The first thing they saw was a group of humans gathered by the water's edge. Something about them seemed strange to Silver Salmon, but he couldn't put his fin on it at first.

'That's it!' he said, turning to Clear-Eyed Salmon. 'Why aren't they carrying nets or fishing rods?'

'They must be the kind who carry cameras instead. The river told us about them, remember: there are humans who carry fishing rods and humans who carry cameras.'

'What's a camera?'

'A machine for taking a photograph.'

The people gathered by the riverside were peering into their cameras, intent on photographing the salmon as they leapt up the rapids.

'Wow, look at that one!'

'What a sight for sore eyes!'

'That one over there is all silver!'

Their excited babble was audible even where Silver Salmon was. He wanted to swim closer to them and show off his silver scales. Clear-Eyed Salmon had said a camera was a machine for taking a photograph; well, then Silver Salmon wanted to be captured by those cameras, to become suspended in time. Excitement bubbled up in him at the thought that there were humans who could be trusted after all.

'What a wonderful world we're living in!' he exclaimed to Clear-Eyed Salmon. She rippled her sides in agreement.

Silver Salmon swims up to the river bank to get a closer look at the kind-hearted humans. As if on cue, they each point their cameras straight at him. Explosions of light detonate from their lenses. This made Silver Salmon jump at first, and the bright lights dazzled him, but he knew he was in no danger. The kind of human who carries a camera was clearly the kind who knows how to look at salmon on their own level.

But then one of the humans catches his eye – one who isn't holding a camera. This human is much smaller than the others, and is sitting by the river's edge with his chin in his hands. His eyes, black and glossy as wild grapes, are staring wonderingly at Silver Salmon. His tiny, pouted lips are mumbling something; he seems to be trying to talk to Silver Salmon.

'You don't have any hair on your face,' Silver Salmon ventures.

'That's because I'm not a grown-up,' the young human said. And Silver Salmon could understand! So there were humans who knew how to speak with their hearts, too!

'Ah,' Silver Salmon said, 'so humans grow hair on their faces when they become adults just like salmon. How did you get here?'

'I came with my dad. That's him in the red jacket. Mum and Big Sis came too.'

So the young human had a father. Silver Salmon

feels a smarting pain in his chest, and regards the young human with envy.

'What sort of man is he, your father?'

'He's a photojournalist.'

'It must be so great for you!'

'What must be?'

'Knowing your father's face.'

'Don't you have a dad?'

'I did, but I never got to meet him. All salmon die after their work at the breeding grounds is done, you see. It's the river who raises us.'

'Well . . . in that case, shouldn't you call the river "Dad"?'

'Really? Just like that?'

'Yeah, definitely.' The young human seems to want to comfort Silver Salmon.

'I have to go now.'

'But I want to talk to you some more.' The sweet little child is reluctant to part from his new friend so soon.

'Little one, there's a favour I want to ask.'

'What is it?'

'I hope that when you're big, you'll be the kind of human who carries a camera. Instead of a fishing rod, that is.'

'OK, I won't forget. Bye.' The little human waves his hand.

'Thank you. Bye!' And Silver Salmon waves his fin as he heads towards the river's upper reaches.

The river is gradually narrowing. Several stones of various sizes have been placed in a line across it.

'Who are you?'

'I'm Stepping Stones,' Stepping Stones answered.

'What are you doing there?' Silver Salmon asked.

'My job is to help people across the river.'

Taking a closer look, Silver Salmon saw the footprints of various people who had walked over Stepping Stones. He even spotted one pair, tiny and with a pretty pattern, that could only belong to the young human he'd just met. Seeing how Stepping Stones had been worn smooth from a combination of the flowing water and humans' feet, Silver Salmon felt sympathetic.

'Doesn't it hurt?'

'I'm fine.'

'Even though humans trample on you with their feet and poke you with their sticks?'

'If they didn't trample on me I'd have no reason to exist. How can I help anyone across the river unless they tread on me?'

'Ah, I see.'

Even Stepping Stones, who looks so plain and innocuous, has a helpful, meaningful job to do, Silver Salmon thought to himself. He enjoys himself even while he's being trampled upon, and all because his purpose in life is clear to him. He puts all his strength into carrying out his allotted task, while also being careful not to obstruct the flow of the river. Compared with him, what a flimsy, meaningless thing I am . . .

Silver Salmon and Clear-Eyed Salmon swim side by side between two of Stepping Stones' stones. The water gets shallower the further up they go, so shallow that their dorsal fins poke out above the surface. This tiny stream is so different from the huge, coursing Green River they knew before that it can't really be called the same thing. But here, Silver Salmon feels a sense of gratification flowing into his body, which he hadn't felt in the deep water.

'Up until now, I always thought the river and the land were completely separate. I thought of the river as the home of salmon and the land as the domain of salmon's enemies, humans. I assumed humans were separate from nature, and from salmon as well. But that was too hasty of me; I see that now. This stream that envelops me is made up of thousands, no, millions of water droplets, which have come down from the very tops of the mountains! Why didn't I realize that this stream is also a part of the great river, that together they flow down to the vast sea?'

Looking down at the stream bed beneath him, Silver Salmon sees how it all interlocks. The land by the water's edge holds hands with the land over which the water flows, forming a single whole.

He thinks of the deep blue sea, of its ceaseless, restless surging. The sea holds hands with all the continents, forming another perfect whole. The land supports the water, the water laps against the land, and so this world is made.

In the shallows of the river's upper reaches, the salmon are busying themselves in preparing to lay eggs. Salmon bustling to and fro in search of the perfect spot, salmon digging up the gravelly river-bed, salmon turning circles over what they've chosen as their patch, warding off would-be interlopers . . . the stream is like a construction site. And indeed, what the salmon are constructing when they spawn – the future – may well be the most important construction of all.

Clear-Eyed Salmon, too, is getting ready to lay eggs. She begins to burrow down into the stream bed with her caudal fin. So absorbed is she in the task of making a spawning site, she is entirely oblivious to the fact that her fin is getting torn on the sharp edge of a stone. She continues burrowing into the gravelly earth, with her ventral fin when her caudal fin has no energy left, then finally, when all her fins are equally exhausted, with her mouth.

'Should I help?' Silver Salmon asked.

'No. You can stay over there.'

'I want to help,' Silver Salmon said, but his muscles were leaden and languid, and his fins felt weighed down. It had taken them such a great amount of time, such a great amount of effort, to get here.

'You can dig for a bit now, if you want.' Clear-Eyed Salmon's mouth is torn and bloodied, like a ragged scrap of cloth. Her breath comes in long sighs, a clear sign of exhaustion. 'Silver Salmon.' Even her eyes, which had always been so clear and bright, have dulled somewhat, irreversibly marked by the passage of time, by the effort she's been forced to expend. She is the very image of a salmon who has passed through the long tunnel known as life. 'Did you find the meaning of life?'

The question embarrasses Silver Salmon. He used to be convinced that there had to be a much weightier reason for living than simply laying eggs. But that great reason he'd agonized over had been nowhere to be found. All he had done, while swimming upriver like the other salmon, was talk with the river, leap over the rapids, and arrive at the upper reaches. There had been no great meaning there.

'All I've realized is that the meaning of life isn't some distant rainbow.'

'Didn't you say there would be hope somewhere?'

'I realized that hope can also be near at hand.'

'In that case, what you're really saying is that, in the end, you couldn't find any specific hope?'

'That's right,' Silver Salmon said, feeling calmer than he ever had before. 'I couldn't find hope. But that isn't something to regret. Compared to salmon whose lives are devoid of even the merest scrap of hope, I think I can say I've been happy. Even now I believe hope exists, somewhere in this world. And that it's there for us to find, as long as we have eyes to see it. My own hope for the future is for many other salmon to think like I do.'

To Clear-Eyed Salmon, Silver Salmon is like someone who has finally returned home after a long journey far away. He wanted to grasp the distant clouds and fleeting rainbows, but now he is content to be what he is – a single salmon. This change of heart seems, to Clear-Eyed Salmon, somewhat sad, but she doesn't blame him for it. Silver Salmon is far more beautiful than all those others, who have never known even the tiniest bit of hope or curiosity. She understands, now, why he was always wanting to poke his head out of the water, to see the world with the eyes of the heart.

'Silver Salmon, it's time for us to lay eggs.' Clear-Eyed Salmon has finished making the site. She looks worn out, but makes an effort to smile. 'Silver Salmon, come here to me,' she says. She seems to want to say his name as many times as possible, perhaps aware that there aren't many opportunities left. Silver Salmon swims up next to her, stopping directly above the site, so that their bodies are aligned side by side. It isn't easy for them to hold themselves still like that. Everything around them seems strangely becalmed, as though time itself has stopped.

'Silver Salmon . . .' Silver Salmon is unable to muster a single word of response. For salmon, laying eggs means the end of life. Silver Salmon feels himself trembling from all the frightening thoughts that are crowding into his mind. But it isn't death itself that he fears. More frightening is that the love he shares with Clear-Eyed Salmon is coming to an end. He is also afraid of being separated from the Green River.

'Clear-Eyed Salmon,' he whispers, 'the river will keep on flowing even after we're gone, right?'

'I think so . . . yes, I think it will flow on.'

'Will the river remember us?'

'I trust it.'

'What does that mean?'

'Only those salmon who trust the river will be able to return to it. Our eggs will trust it too, I'm sure.' Clear-Eyed Salmon's words are composed. But Silver Salmon can't conceal the sense of unease lapping like waves in a corner of his heart.

'When we're gone, will the river take care of our eggs?'

'Even though we salmon don't raise our eggs, our death ensures that they're provided for. There's no doubt in my mind that the river will look after them.'

Everything is growing dark in front of Silver Salmon's eyes. If it were possible for this thing known as life to be turned back, he wants to start again from the beginning. If such a thing were possible, he would have devoted himself to making many more beautiful, happy memories for Clear-Eyed Salmon than he had done this time round. If only the clock hand of life, where so much time had been wasted in shame and fruitless searching, could be turned back . . .

'When our children hatch from the eggs, we'll be forgotten, as if we never existed, no?'

'But perhaps it's only by forgetting us that our children will be able to make happy memories for themselves. That's just how life is for salmon.' As soon as she finishes speaking, Clear-Eyed Salmon opens her mouth as wide as it can possibly go.

Hundreds of eggs rush out of her stomach, their rich cherry hue resembling that of her own body. Each egg sinks down to the riverbed and settles among the gravel.

Now it's Silver Salmon's turn. He closes his eyes tight and a white fluid streams out from beneath his stomach, drenching each of the cherry-coloured eggs.

Silver Salmon and Clear-Eyed Salmon remain as they are for a few moments, side by side and unmoving, with their mouths gaping open. It is both the first and last scene in this world that the two of them have achieved together. The most sublime, and also the saddest.

It was all in order to achieve this single scene that they cast their tender young bodies down over the rapids five years ago. It was for this that they struggled against the rough waves of the Bering Sea in the North Pacific. For this, they made the long and arduous journey back to the Green River, risking death at every turn. Precisely in order to achieve this scene, the scene of death solemnized by the creation of new life, they overcame countless deaths.

Only once the spawning has finished will the souls depart their bodies, all the energy that has animated their lives flowing back into the world. Leached of colour, their bodies will float to the top of the river and bob gently on the surface.

Silver Salmon and Clear-Eyed Salmon.

Perhaps, before they close their eyes, they take one last long look at each other and say something like this:

'Those eggs will have your clear eyes.'

'Perhaps those clear eyes are already peering into the water of the North Pacific.'

And.

Winter will come to the Green River.

When it does, the water at the bottom of the river will continue to flow, under a quilt formed of huge ice slabs. That quilt will stay in place all winter long, while the river raises the salmon eggs nestled snug in its bosom. Now and then, a passer-by will toss a stone at those slabs of blue-tinged ice capping the Green River, causing a cracking sound to ring out.

Until the spring comes, be careful; remember there are young salmon there, growing up in the deep heart of the river.

Salmon: the very word is heady with the scent of the rushing river.